Stormy Night

MICHÈLE LEMIEUX

Stormy Night

MICHÈLE LEMIEUX

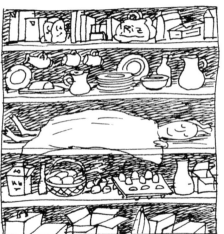

KIDS CAN PRESS

For Darcia

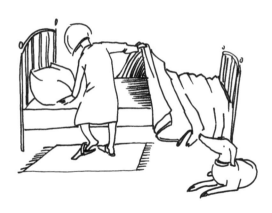

I can't sleep!
Too many questions are buzzing through my head.

Where does infinity end?

If someone made a hole in the sky,
would we see infinity?
And if we made a hole in that hole,
what would we see?

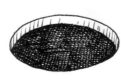

Is there life on other planets?

Imagine if someone from another planet
were hiding here among us!

Where do we come from?

Who decided what the first human would look like?

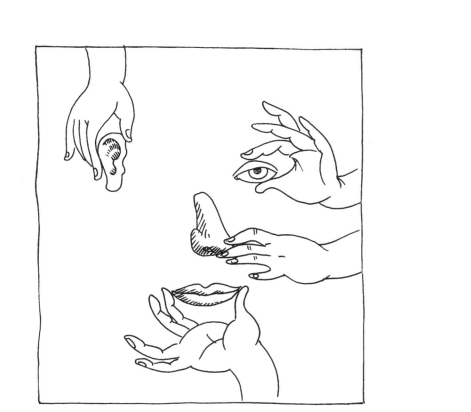

Imagine if we grew out of the ground like vegetables ...

... or if we were manufactured ...

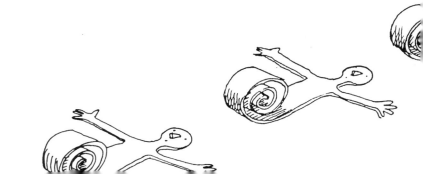

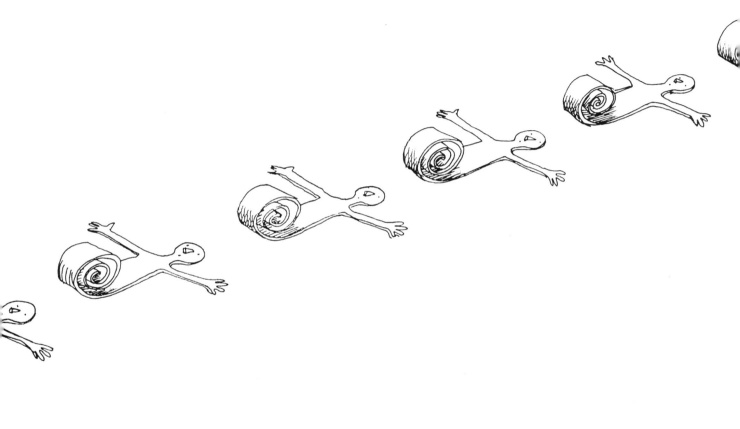

... or made from recycled parts!

Will I have children someday?

Who am I?

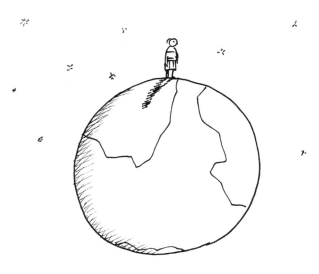

Is there only one of me in the world?

Am I nice looking?

Am I likable? And smart?

Does Fido think he's good looking?

Sometimes I feel like I don't fit in my body!

Imagine if we could switch bodies ...

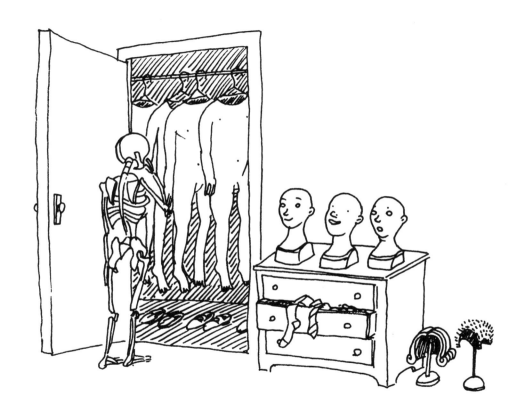

... or at least hide the parts we don't like!

And if we could switch bodies, would someone choose mine?

Sometimes I feel completely lost!

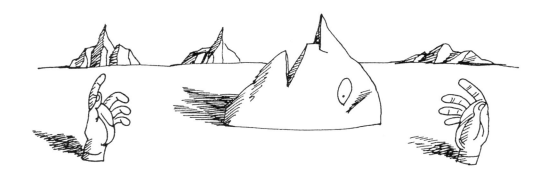

When that happens, I want to be cuddled like a baby.

And then there are other times when I wish
the whole world would just leave me alone,
so I can really do what I want to do!

When I'm happy, I feel as if I'm filled with light.

When I'm angry, I explode!

When I cry, it feels as if the tide's coming in!

Will I be a hero someday?

Will my name be in the encyclopedia?

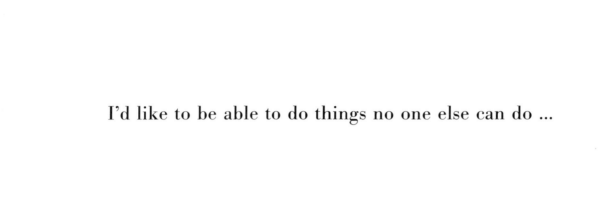

I'd like to be able to do things no one else can do ...

My brother and sister would die of envy!

Everyone would admire me!

Is my whole life already worked out in advance?

Or will I have to find my way all by myself?

Fido always finds his way back, even when we get lost!

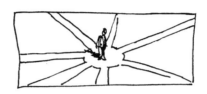

Will I always make the right decisions?
And how will I know if they're right?

Will I always be able to avoid pitfalls?

Is there anyone watching over me?

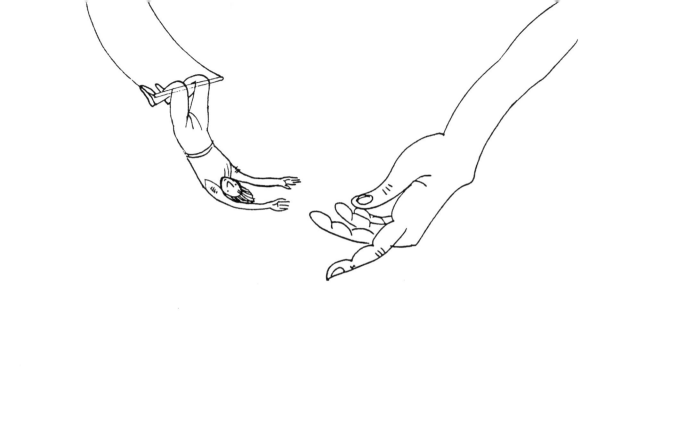

Besides Mom, who always thinks of everything!

What exactly is fate?

And chance, who is behind it?

Where do all of the ideas that float through my head come from?
And where do they go when they leave my head?

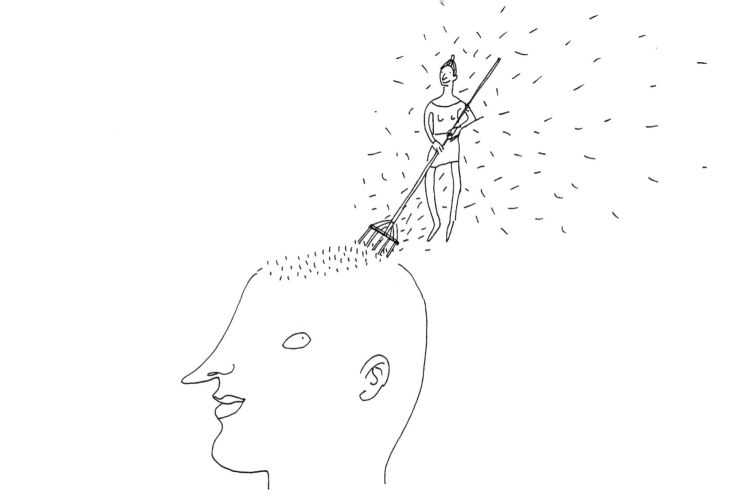

Sometimes I have absolutely nothing in my head!

Like when I'm asked to draw a picture for Aunt Elsie.

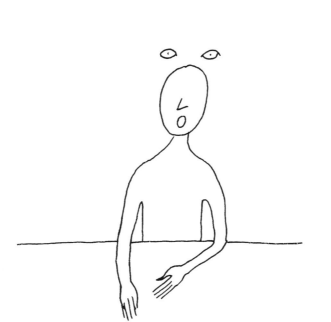

Sometimes I feel as if my eyes can see inside of me.

Dad once told me about a man who lived completely in his imagination.

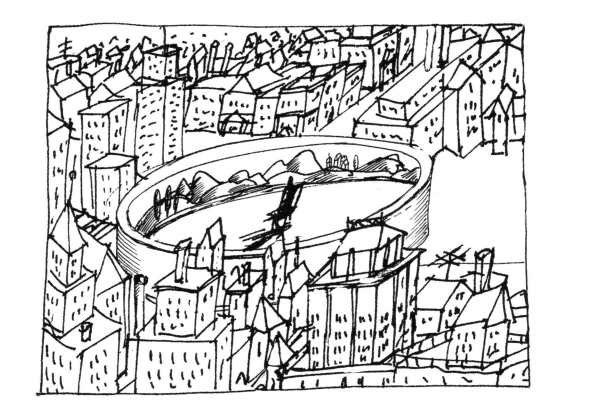

What about me — do I have an imagination?

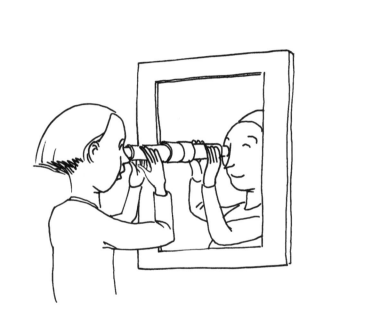

I'd like to invent things that don't yet exist!

Maybe I'm talented and I don't even know it?

When I dream at night ...

... where am I?

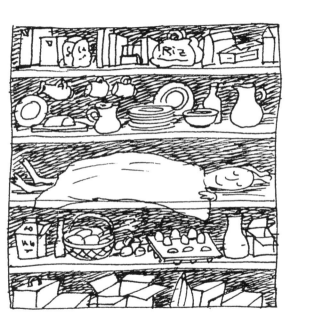

Maybe on another planet?

A planet where we all meet when we dream!

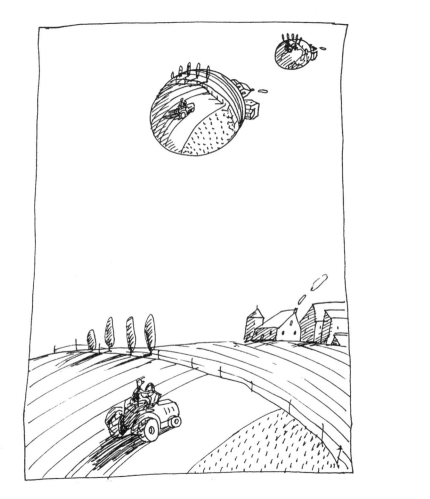

And what if life were just a dream ...
and dreams at night were really real?

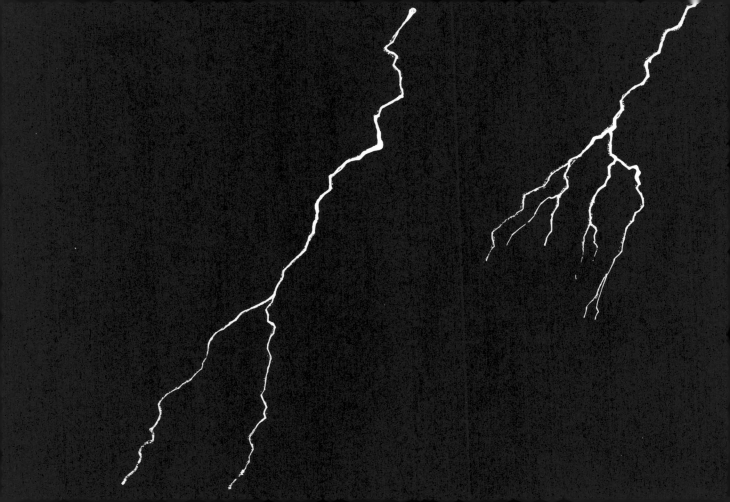

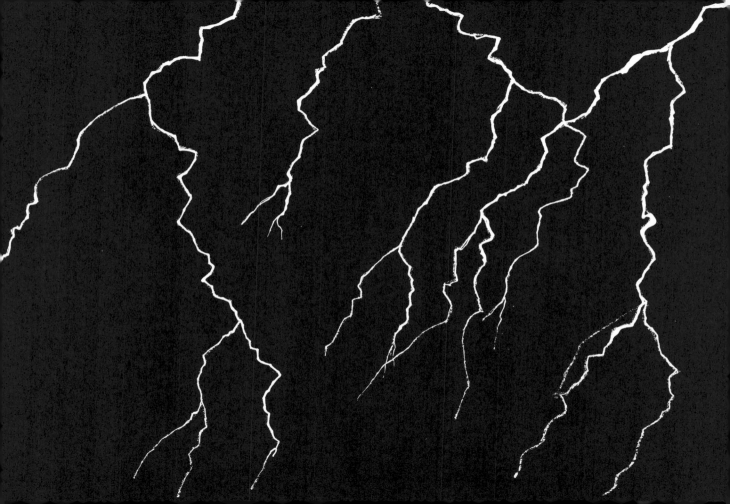

I'm scared!

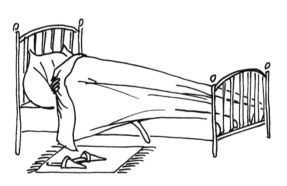

Stay with me, Fido!

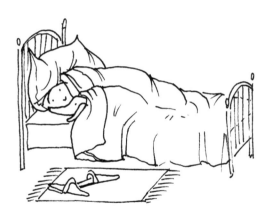

At night I feel all alone and unprotected.

I'm scared of being abandoned ...

... of being separated from everyone I love ...

... of being left all alone in the world!

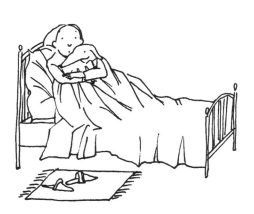

I'm afraid that nobody loves me!

I'm scared of war!

Mom!

I'm afraid of robbers,

of wild beasts and monsters,

and maniacs!

I'm afraid of what lies ahead of me in life!

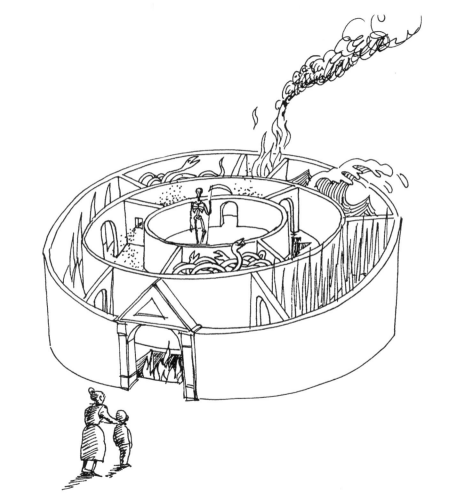

Will the world come to an end someday?

Will I know when it's time to die?

Will it hurt?

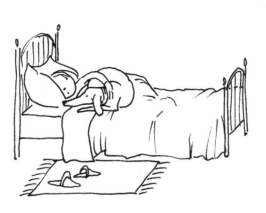

When death comes to get me,
I'll hide so well that it won't find me!

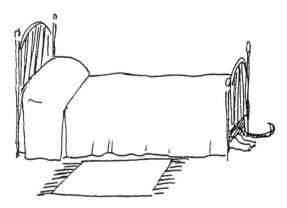

Can we each see our own soul?

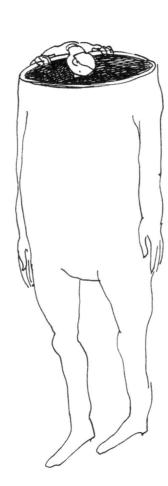

Where does it go when we die?
Maybe it will join infinity!

But where does infinity end?
On the other side of the sky?

Does God live there?
Do we go through there when we die?

So many people have died already — will I be able to find the people I knew in such a crowd?

Are things better after death than in life?
What do you do there all day long?

And hell — does it really exist?

Mr. Pratt, our old neighbor, was an unhappy man. He used to say his life was hell on earth!

After I die, maybe everything will be just the way it was before I was born!

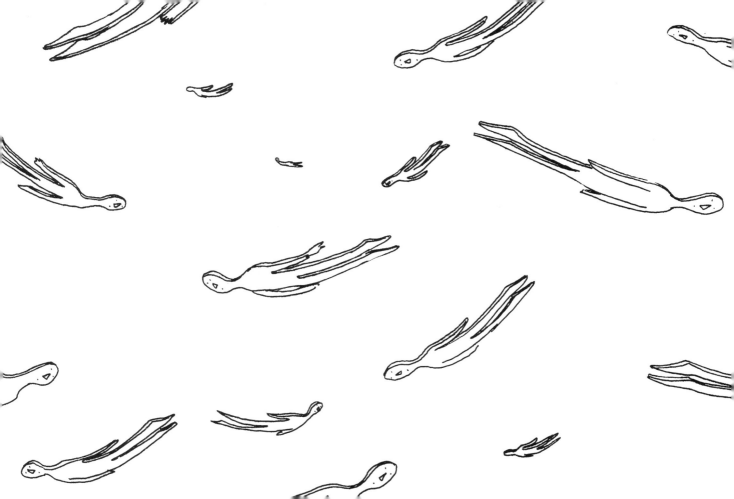

What if death simply erases our memory,
so that we can start over somewhere else?

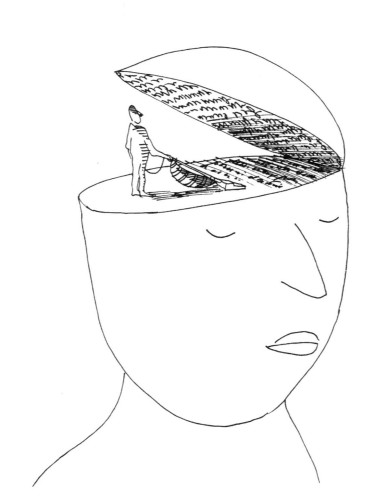

And what if we came back to earth in another form!

Imagine if it showed!

But if all the people, all the animals, all the plants,
all the shells and all the insects were reborn,
there wouldn't be any room left in heaven
or on earth, would there?

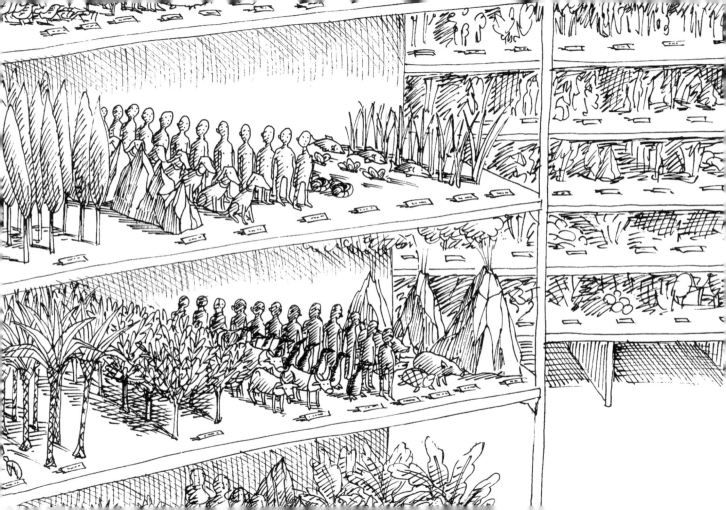

And what if there's nothing after death?

I'm hungry!

And what if we could live forever ...

... ending up by understanding   all mysteries,

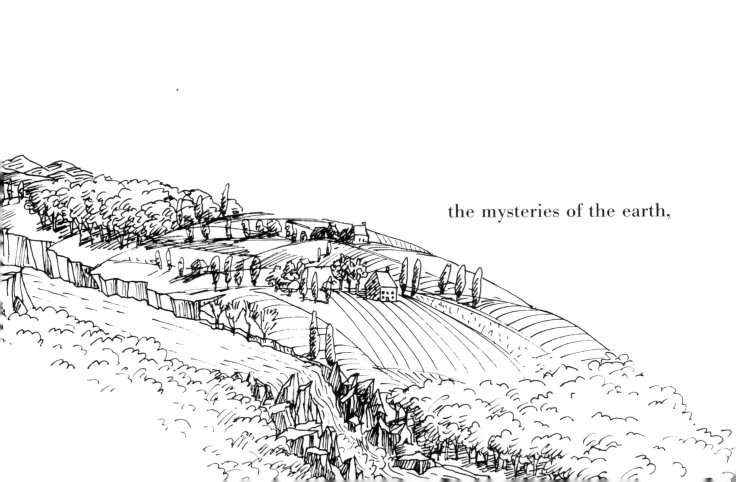

the mysteries of the earth,

nd of all the universe,

and I would have friends everywhere!

Wouldn't that be great!

First North American edition 1999
Copyright © 1996 by Michèle Lemieux

Published in Germany by Beltz & Gelberg under the title *Gewitternacht*
English translation copyright © 1999 by Michèle Lemieux

With thanks to David Shewan for his assistance with the English translation

Published in Canada by   Published in the U.S. by
Kids Can Press Ltd.   Kids Can Press Ltd.
29 Birch Avenue   4500 Witmer Estates
Toronto, ON M4V 1E2   Niagara Falls, NY 14305-1386

Cover design by Angela Grauerholz
Interior design by Angela Grauerholz and Judith Poirier.
Printed and bound in Hong Kong by Book Art Inc.

CM 99 0 9 8 7 6 5 4 3 2

Canadian Cataloguing in Publication Data

Lemieux, Michèle, 1955–
      [Gewitternacht. English]
      Stormy Night

Translation of: Gewitternacht.
ISBN 1-55074-692-8

I. Title. II. Title: Gewitternacht. English.

PS8573.E546G5813 1999   jC833   C99-930579-4
PZ7.L53738St 1999

Kids Can Press is a Nelvana company.